ETERNAL
ZACHARY'S STORY

CYNTHIA LEITICH SMITH
ILLUSTRATED BY MING DOYLE

CANDLEWICK PRESS

MY GIRL IS SLEEPING IN THE SHADOW OF DEATH.

I HAVE TO BE VIGILANT. PROTECT HER.

"FOR, I AM SURE, YOU HAVE YOUR HANDS FULL ALL . . . ALL . . ."

MIRANDA KNOWS HER LINES. SHE'S JUST NERVOUS. BUT THIS AUDITION IS A BUST.

OH, MY GOD! SHE'S HORRIBLE!

SHH!

VIDEO CITY

NEW RELEASES

LUCY AND MIRANDA ARE LIFELONG PALS. LUCY HAS HAD A THING FOR THE CLERK, KURT, FOR A WHILE.

IF Y'ALL ARE UP FOR IT, I HAVE A SCARY IDEA.

ME? I, UM, I HAVE CURFEW AT—

YOU'RE SPENDING THE NIGHT.

ME AND THIS FRIEND OF MINE, SOMETIMES WE KICK BACK A FEW BREWS AT THE OLD CEMETERY NEAR THE HIGH SCHOOL.

MY PARENTS TRUST ME, AND THEY'RE HEAVY SLEEPERS.

THEY SAY THE DEAD WALK THERE AT MIDNIGHT.

I HATE THE SOUND OF THAT.

YOU KNOW BETTER THAN TO REVEAL YOURSELF! AND IN FULL GLORY! YOU CHANGED THE NATURAL ORDER.

YOU BID THE FIEND IN.

FIEND?

MIRANDA SHEN MCALLISTER SHOULD BE IN MY CHARGE. MY CARE. BUT NOW HER VERY SOUL IS FORFEIT.

I—

YOU HAVE INTERFERED. YOU WILL BOTH PAY THE PENALTY.

THE ARCHANGEL, MY WINGS, AND MY GIRL ARE GONE.

WHAT WAS THAT SOUND? LUCY?

CAN YOU WALK?

COUGH.

THANK YOU, WHOEVER YOU ARE. MY FRIEND MIRANDA . . .

SHE'S GONE. WE'VE LOST HER.

I SEARCHED FOR KURT, FOR ANSWERS . . .

BUT FOUND . . . NOTHING.

11

AT FIRST, I DID OKAY. I VOLUNTEERED AT A YOUTH SHELTER, BUT I COULDN'T SAVE THEM ALL.

THEN AFTER I MET A GIRL WHO LOOKED TOO MUCH LIKE MIRANDA . . .

I GAVE IT UP AND HITCHED A RIDE SOUTH.

IF YOU HAD TO BE HOMELESS AND DAMNED, THE WEATHER AND POLITICS IN AUSTIN WERE BETTER FOR IT.

ZACHARY? BUDDY?

DID YOU DRINK TEQUILA OR BATHE IN IT?

WHOEVER BROUGHT ME HERE, I COULD USE A BOTTLE OF WATER, A SHOWER, FRESH CLOTHES, AND A CLUE.

YOU DON'T ASK FOR MUCH, DO YOU?

MY BEST FRIEND, JOSHUA.

MAN, I'VE MISSED YOU!

NOT THAT I'M NOT GLAD TO SEE YOU. BUT WHY ARE YOU HERE?

13

I'VE BEEN—

IT DOESN'T MATTER WHERE YOU'VE BEEN. IT'S ALL ABOUT WHERE YOU'RE GOING.

OH, PLEASE. ENOUGH WITH THE CRYPTIC CRAP.

WHAT IS THAT?

IT'S A TATTOO. OF A CHERUB.

THAT IS NOT ONE OF THE CHERUBIM! THAT IS A FAT, NAKED WHITE BABY WITH WINGS!

HOW COULD YOU DO THAT? BODY. TEMPLE. DIDN'T YOU READ THE WRITTEN?

I'VE DONE WORSE.

MIRANDA'S NAME HANGS UNSPOKEN BETWEEN US.

WHY ARE YOU HERE, JOSH?

MICHAEL SENT ME WITH A REQUEST. HE CALLED IT "AN ASSASSINATION OF SORTS." IF YOU SUCCEED, KEEP THE FAITH, AND REMAIN VIRTUOUS, YOU MIGHT GET REINSTATED.

MICHAEL WANTS ME TO KILL—

WIPE OUT.

SOMEONE—

SOMETHING. SOMETHING OF TREMENDOUS SIGNIFICANCE. WHAT DO YOU SAY?

IS THAT ALL YOU'RE GOING TO TELL ME?

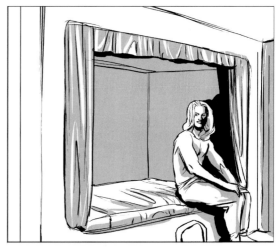

YEAH, YEAH, OKAY! NICE SEEING YOU.

STILL . . .

AFTER ALL THAT'S HAPPENED, IT'S NICE TO KNOW THAT JOSH IS STILL JOSH.

Tia Leticia's
SALSA BAR
42 Whitby Estates
Chicago, Illinois

CHICAGO, ILLINOIS

EXCUSE ME, FATHER?

YES?

I'M LOST. I WAS SUPPOSED TO GET ON A NORTHBOUND TRAIN AND—

WHERE ARE YOU TRYING TO GO?

WHITBY ESTATES.

THE TRAINS DON'T STOP THERE. NOT ANYMORE. ONE OF OUR MORE SUBTLE VICTORIES.

WHAT'S THAT SUPPOSED TO MEAN?

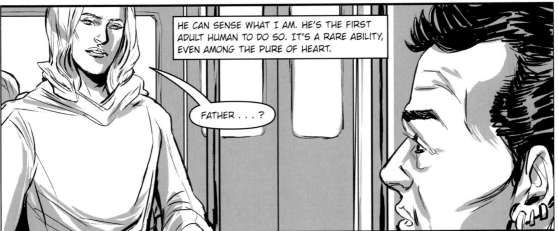

HE CAN SENSE WHAT I AM. HE'S THE FIRST ADULT HUMAN TO DO SO. IT'S A RARE ABILITY, EVEN AMONG THE PURE OF HEART.

FATHER . . . ?

RAMOS.

TAKE A CAB. TELL THE DRIVER TO DROP YOU OFF A BLOCK AWAY.

IF HE BALKS, OFFER A FIFTY-PERCENT TIP UP FRONT.

YOU'RE GOING DRESSED LIKE THAT?

I GUESS.

MY CARD. JUST IN CASE.

FATHER RAMOS †

MAY I HELP YOU?

CAN I HAVE FOUR EGG ROLLS TO GO? AND WHERE'S YOUR MEN'S ROOM?

FATHER RAMOS APPARENTLY THINKS I SHOULD DRESS TO IMPRESS. AND JOSHUA GAVE ME THESE DUDS FOR A REASON.

男
MEN

20

HALF AN HOUR LATER

I'M HEADED TO WHITBY ESTATES.

UH, JOSHUA?

FORGET IT. HE'LL SHOW WHEN HE WANTS TO. OR WHEN MICHAEL OKAYS IT.

WHITBY ESTATES, AND I'LL TIP YOU—

GET IN. NO EXTRA CHARGE.

YOU'RE SURE?

IT IS OKAY. I AM GOOD WITH GOD.

I NEED TO MAKE A QUICK STOP ON THE WAY. DO YOU KNOW WHERE I COULD BUY A—

WEAPON? FOR WHERE YOU'RE GOING?

IF I EVER MAKE IT BACK UPSTAIRS, I OWE THIS GUY'S GUARDIAN ANGEL A BEER.

I'VE STILL GOT THE CROSS UNDER MY SHIRT AND THE STAKE UP MY SLEEVE.

THE ADDRESS IS . . .

ARRoOOoo.

HERE.

THOSE RED EYES . . . THEY'RE NOT WOLVES. NOT WEREWOLVES.

THEY'RE VAMPIRES IN WOLF FORM.

WHAT I WOULDN'T GIVE FOR A FLAMING SWORD.

WHO'RE YOU? ARE YOU HERE ABOUT THE JOB?

JOB?

SURE.

AND YOUR NAME?

ZACHARY.

WHERE'S YOUR RÉSUMÉ?

I DON'T HAVE ONE WITH ME.

YOUR LAST NAME?

WHO'RE YOU?

VALID POINT. FURTHERMORE, WHY SHOULD I BE REDUCED TO BABYSITTING?

WHATEVER THAT MEANS, HE DOESN'T SAY IT LIKE HE REALLY MINDS.

FOLLOW ME. CHOP, CHOP.

THOSE AREN'T ANIMAL HEADS. THEY CAME OFF OF SHAPE-SHIFTERS.

DON'T TAKE IT PERSONALLY. THE MAIDS DON'T SAY MUCH.

HE LOOKS SIGNIFICANT.

WHO'S THAT?

YOU DON'T KNOW? WELL, THIS SHOULD BE AMUSING. YOU'LL FIND OUT SOON ENOUGH.

A VAMPIRE IN BAT FORM. AND THE GIRL, IT CAN'T BE . . .

I TOLD HER TO STAY AWAY FROM THE CASTLE!

BANG!

MIRANDA!

IN THE BOWL . . . IT'S BLOOD.

HAVE A SEAT.

HOW MANY PEOPLE HAS SHE KILLED? DRAINED?

YOUR NAME.

WHAT ABOUT IT?

WHAT IS IT?

SHE'S TRIPPING.

MY INSTINCT IS . . .

TO CATCH HER.

ARE YOU A SHAPE-SHIFTER?

I'M ZACHARY. AND NO, I'M NOT A SHIFTER.

YOU'RE HERE FOR THE JOB?

YOU COULD SAY THAT.

SHE'S FLUSTERED. ATTRACTED?

WERE YOU REFERRED, OR DID YOU SEE THE JOB ANNOUNCEMENT?

I WAS REFERRED.

BY?

I WAS AFRAID SHE'D ASK THAT.

JOSHUA. JOSHUA MICHAELS.

AS MY PERSONAL ASSISTANT, YOU WOULD BE EXPECTED TO DO MY BIDDING. EVERYTHING FROM ANSWERING THE PHONE TO ACTING AS MY LIAISON TO PROTECTING MY SAFETY TO . . .

TO?

ATTENTING TO MY PERSONAL NEEDS.

I'LL TAKE IT.

IT'S NOT UP TO YOU TO TAKE IT. IT'S UP TO ME TO OFFER IT. I MEAN, ME. I MEAN, MYSELF.

VERY FLUSTERED.

YOU'RE IN LUCK, ZACHARY. AS IT HAPPENS, WITH THE MASTER ABROAD, I HAVE MANY PRESSING RESPONSIBILITIES.

THE MASTER? *HE'S* THE FIEND IN THE PORTRAIT. THE ONE WHO DID THIS TO HER.

I'M WILLING TO TAKE YOU ON. ON, UM, A TRIAL BASIS. HARRISON WILL SHOW YOU AROUND.

WHATEVER YOU SAY, MIRANDA.

WELCOME TO STAFF DRACUL. YOUR OFFICIAL TITLE IS "PERSONAL ASSISTANT TO THE MISTRESS," OFTEN CALLED "PRINCESS" OR "HER ROYAL HIGHNESS."

DRACUL? AS IN "DRACULA"?

EXPLAINS THE CASTLE. TALK ABOUT BUYING INTO YOUR OWN PRESS.

THE MASTER IS NOT DRACULA PRIME, THE FIRST DRACULA. HE IS ARCHIBALD MOSBY RADFORD, ORIGINALLY OF THE VIRGINIA RADFORDS.

IT HAS SIMPLY BECOME CUSTOMARY TO REFER TO THE CURRENT ETERNAL REGENT AS "THE DRACULA."

BORROWED GLORY.

YOU MAY REFER TO HIM AS "MASTER" OR "HIS ROYAL MAJESTY."

LIKE HELL.

SPEAK TO ETERNALS ONLY WHEN SPOKEN TO. THAT INCLUDES THE SENTRIES. AVOID THE V-WORD AT ALL COSTS.

V AS IN "VAMPIRE"?

THESE ARE *SERVANTS'* QUARTERS?

WE PREFER "EXECUTIVE ADMINISTRATIVE STAFF."

YOU'LL NEED MORE CLOTHES, INCLUDING PARTY CLOTHES. IT'S UP TO THE MISTRESS TO DECIDE IF SHE WANTS TO DRESS YOU OR FOR YOU TO DRESS AT ALL AND WHETHER TO UPGRADE YOUR ROOM. THE MASTER UPGRADED MINE.

WHERE IS THIS MASTER OF YOURS?

ABROAD FOR THE MONTH. HE LEFT TWO DAYS AGO.

I'LL HAVE TO BIDE MY TIME UNTIL THE VAMPIRE KING RETURNS.

LATER

SSSSSss

INTERESTING.

IT'S A LIST OF COMMONLY USED CASTLE PHRASES.
"DINNER IS SERVED."
"THE MASTER/MISTRESS WILL SEE YOU NOW."
"PRESENTING FILL-IN-THE-NAME-OF-THE-ETERNAL."

MAYBE IT'S STANDARD TRAINING MATERIAL.
OR MAYBE—FOR A HUMAN SERVING THE
UNDEAD—HARRISON'S NOT SUCH A BAD GUY.

AN ETERNAL, THEO, AWAITS THE PRINCESS'S AUDIENCE IN THE PARLOR.

HERE'S HIS FILE.

KNOK

ENTER.

VAMP TO SEE YOU.

SUCH STRIKING GREEN EYES. I COULD SCOOP THEM OUT AND PUT THEM IN GLASS PAPERWEIGHTS. ONE FOR YOU AND ONE FOR ME. YOU COULD CONSIDER YOURS A PARTING GIFT.

WHAT'S YOUR POINT?

NOT "VAMP" OR "VAMPIRE." "ETERNAL."

ONLY BECAUSE YOU ARE IN TRAINING WILL I TOLERATE THE OCCASIONAL SLIP AND ONLY FOR AS LONG AS I'M SO INCLINED.

IT'S STUPID, BUT I'M MAD AT HER. MAD AT HER FOR DYING. MAD AT HER FOR BEING THIS THING. MAD ENOUGH TO PUSH MY LUCK AND JEOPARDIZE MY MISSION.

LISTEN UP, MIRANDA, I DON'T KNOW . . .

THEO

JOSH BRIEFLY MATERIALIZES TO WARN ME TO CAN THE ATTITUDE.

FINE. I'LL BE GOOD.

YOU LISTEN. THE TONE AND TEMPERAMENT OF CASTLE LIFE IS PRISTINE, ORDERLY, SEDATE, AND REGAL. FATHER HAS ASKED THAT IN HIS ABSENCE—

FATHER?

THE EXALTED MASTER. FATHER HAS ASKED THAT I MAINTAIN THE STATUS QUO, DEAL WITH ANY VISITORS.

OUR PRIORITY IS PLANNING HIS DEATHDAY GALA. WE'LL WORK ON THAT TOGETHER.

BUT FIRST, THEO.

THEO

I NEED YOU TO TAKE THEO'S REMAINS TO THE CREMATORIUM IN THE DUNGEON.

WHAT DID HE DO?

DO?

THEO.

OH, WELL, HE TRIED TO KILL A HUMAN GIRL, WHICH . . . HOW ABOUT WE JUST SAY IT'S COMPLICATED?

HUH.

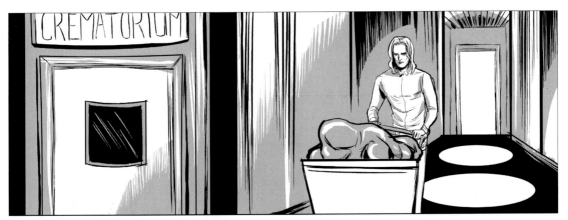

CREMATORIUM

THEY'RE KEEPING HUMAN PRISONERS.

HOW CAN I PLAY SERVANT, WITH THIS GOING ON?

DAMN YOU. DAMN YOU.

I WISH I COULD TELL HIM WHAT I AM. WHY I'M HERE.

ABOUT THE PUNCTURE MARKS. THE ETERNALS DON'T KILL THE PRISONERS?

DEPENDS. WE GOT SYRINGES THAT WORK AS GOOD AS FANGS. BUT IF THEY GET SICK, WE BURN THE WHOLE BLEEDING STOCK. THE MASTER DOESN'T LIKE TO TAKE CHANCES WHEN IT COMES TO PHLEGM.

IT'S DANGEROUS TO HIM?

NAH, IT JUST GROSSES HIM OUT.

EXCELLENT. I'VE JUST RULED OUT MUCUS AS A WEAPON.

DON'T SWEAT IT, PAL. NOBODY BUT THE PRINCESS HERSELF IS GONNA TAKE A BITE OUT OF YOU.

43

WE SHOULD MOVE TO THE FORMAL DINING HALL. ON THE WAY, YOU CAN PICK UP YOUR MEAL AND FETCH ME—

QUITE A DUNGEON YOU'VE GOT.

SOMETHING YOU'D LIKE TO SAY?

IT DOESN'T BOTHER YOU, THE PEOPLE DOWNSTAIRS? THE WAY YOU USE THEM?

I'M SURE THIS IS ALL OVERWHELMING AT FIRST.

WHAT YOU MUST UNDERSTAND IS THAT THOSE HUMANS IN THE DUNGEON ARE THERE FOR A REASON. IT'S THEIR NATURAL ROLE.

HOW DO YOU KNOW?

I KNOW. I KNOW MANY THINGS. THINK OF WHAT I COULD SHOW YOU, WHAT WE COULD DO TOGETHER.

IS SHE HITTING ON ME? AFTER WHAT I JUST SAW?

HAVE YOU VISITED THEM? TALKED TO THEM? THEY'RE JUST KIDS.

WE SHOULD SPEAK OF THE FUTURE. OUR FUTURE. THERE ARE CASTLE ROOMS WE'VE YET TO VISIT.

I'M TALKING ABOUT THE DUNGEON.

NOBODY ELSE WANTS THOSE HUMANS. THEY'RE ONLY GOOD FOR THEIR BLOOD.

AGAIN, HOW DO YOU KNOW?

NOBODY ENDS UP HERE BY ACCIDENT.

ARE YOU TALKING ABOUT THEM OR YOURSELF?

PRESS 1 FOR MIRANDA, 2 FOR ME, AND 3 FOR NORA, THE CHEF.

HER ROYAL MAJESTY'S PLATINUM CARD. YOU CAN USE IT TO ORDER THE NEW FURNITURE FOR HER OFFICE. AND WHATEVER ELSE SHE NEEDS.

SWEET.

THE DUNGEON

WHAT'S ALL THAT?

LONG UNDERWEAR. ORDERS FROM UPSTAIRS. THE HOSPITAL GOWNS ARE A LITTLE TIRED.

THANK . . . THANK YOU.

I WISH I COULD GIVE THEM SOME HOPE TO GO ALONG WITH THE POLYESTER.

GIMME, MAN.

WHAT'S THIS? YOU PLAYIN' US?

I CAN'T BLAME THEM FOR BEING SUSPICIOUS.

GTAWWWRRK!

HARRISON? LAST TIME I SAW HIM, HE WAS HUMAN. NOT ANYMORE.

HE'S CONSUMED BY BLOODLUST.

TOO FAST TO OUTRUN. NO PLACE TO HIDE.

CLANK!

THE LOCK'S BEEN BROKEN FOR A LONG TIME, BUT DON'T TELL HIM THAT. . . .

GAH!

NO!

SO MUCH FOR DUNGEON MANAGER GUS.

WHO ARE YOU?

BRENEK.

HELLO, NORA? BAD NEWS. HARRISON'S UNDEAD.

IN THE KITCHEN

NORA SAID—

HARRISON TOOK THE TUNNEL TO THE GROUNDS. THE SENTRIES WILL INTERCEPT HIM.

I DON'T KNOW ABOUT THAT.

MIRANDA SEEMS SHOCKED. EITHER DRAC RADFORD DIDN'T TELL HER THAT HE'D FED HIS OWN BLOOD TO HARRISON OR SOMEONE ELSE TURNED HIM.

COULD'VE BEEN A SENTRY.

DID YOU CALL THE ENFORCERS?

THE WHAT?

THE MASTER'S EXECUTIONERS.

NEVER MIND. I'LL DO IT MYSELF.

NO RUSH.

THE FOLLOWING EVENING

TRY THE WHITE TUX NEXT!

I'M NOT IN A BARBERSHOP QUARTET.

YOU'RE NOT TO ARGUE. YOU'RE TO OBEY.

WHATEVER YOU SAY, YOUR HIGHNESS.

THE COATS ARE ALL TOO TIGHT THROUGH THE SHOULDERS.

THAT'S YOUR FAULT FOR HAVING THE BODY OF A COMIC-BOOK SUPERHERO.

MIRANDA, DO YOU SMELL –?

OH, MY GOD! ZACHARY!

YOU WOULD THINK VAMPS WOULD USE FLAME-RETARDANT FABRIC.

ARE THESE ENCHANTED CANDLES?

IT'S POSSIBLE. WE GET A LOT OF MAGICAL CATALOGS. YOU KNOW HOW IT IS WHEN YOUR NAME GETS ON A LIST.

DON'T YOU HAVE A SPRINKLER SYSTEM?

TOO DANGEROUS. SOMEONE COULD BLESS THE WATER.

THERE'S SUPPOSED TO BE A FIRE EXTINGUISHER IN EVERY ROOM.

NORA! FIRE IN THE NURSERY!

COME ON!

THAT CANDELABRUM DOESN'T BELONG BY THE DRAPES. IT'S ALWAYS TOWARD THE BACK OF THE ROOM.

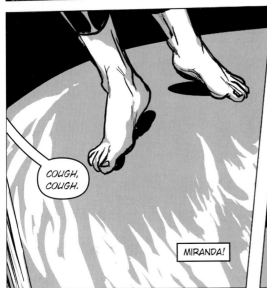

COUGH, COUGH.

MIRANDA!

SHOULDN'T WE CALL THE FIRE DEPARTMENT?

WE CAN'T. THEN EVERYONE WOULD FIND OUT. FATHER WOULD FIND OUT.

FINE.

KOF
KOF KOF

IS IT OUT?

YEAH. ARE YOU OKAY?

I'M IN CHARGE FOR FIVE MEASLY DAYS, AND LOOK AT ALL THAT'S GONE WRONG! FATHER WILL BE SO DISAPPOINTED.

HE'S ALL I HAVE.

NO. SHE STILL HAS ME.

HAVE YOU HEARD FROM MIRANDA?

SHE STAYED IN THE WINE CELLAR LAST NIGHT. AND SHE'S USUALLY OUT AND ABOUT BY NOW. SHE'S ALSO FASTING, WHICH IS DANGEROUS.

TWO NIGHTS LATER, THE CASTLE KITCHEN

DON'T WORRY, BOY. YOU'LL LURE HER UPSTAIRS SOON ENOUGH. YOU'RE THE BEST EYE CANDY THIS PRETENTIOUS MAUSOLEUM HAS SEEN IN AGES.

JUST OUT OF CURIOSITY, DOES DRAC RADFORD EVER SAMPLE ANY OF YOUR COOKING?

IT'S A CHALLENGE FOR HIM, BEING AN ETERNAL, TO EAT SOLID FOOD. BUT HE'S WORKED PAST HIS GAG REFLEX AND CAN KEEP DOWN A LIGHT MEAL.

IT WAS QUITE THE MOMENT WHEN HE ENJOYED HIS FIRST BITE OF RHUBARB PIE SINCE THE CIVIL WAR.

I DON'T SEE WHY HE'D BOTHER. THEY'RE NOT CALLED BLOODSUCKERS FOR NOTHING.

THE MASTER HASN'T FORGOTTEN THE JOYS OF HIS HUMAN LIFE. NOW AND THEN, HE WANTS A TASTE, SO TO SPEAK, OF THE WORLD HE LEFT BEHIND. IT COULD BE THAT HE MISSES IT.

WHY DO YOU THINK HE PICKED MIRANDA TO BECOME HIS PRINCESS?

AS A HUMAN, HE HAD DAUGHTERS OF HIS OWN. MAYBE HE MISSED BEING A FATHER, TOO.

I HOPE MIRANDA'S NOT TOO FREAKED OUT.

THE PRINCESS? FREAKED-OUT ETERNALS ARE—

THE MASTER, SURE. BUT MIRANDA'S JUST A BABY. A BABY VIPER, BUT A BABY NONETHELESS.

YES, SHE'S CERTAINLY PRECIOUS. UNLESS YOU'RE THE ONE WITHIN STRIKING RANGE.

LAURIE, THE CHAUFFEUR, IS A LITTLE SKITTISH. NOT THAT I BLAME HER UNDER THE CIRCUMSTANCES.

HOW GRACIOUS OF HER TO SPEND THE EVENING IN HER COFFIN. I'LL BE IN THE GARAGE, UM, ROTATING THE TIRES.

LAURIE?

OH, LEAVE HER BE. IT'S BETTER THAT SHE STAY ALERT. MIND THAT THERE'S A LESSON IN HER EXAMPLE.

LAURIE MENTIONED MIRANDA'S COFFIN.

IN THE CELLAR.

THE PRINCESS AND MASTER EACH HAVE THEIR OWN.

IF YOU WANT TO MEET IN YOUR OFFICE TONIGHT, IT'S ALL SPICK-AND-SPAN.

I'VE BEEN HELPING NORA OUT IN THE KITCHEN, AND I THOUGHT YOU MIGHT BE THIRSTY.

WHAT'S THIS? IT SMELLS LIKE . . . IT'S NOT HUMAN.

IT'S COW BLOOD.

I EXPECT HER TO OBJECT.

SHE DOESN'T.

NOT LONG AFTERWARD

PRESENTING SABINE AND PHILIPPE.

THEY'RE SURPRISE GUESTS. ARISTOCRATS. AND THEY'RE IN TROUBLE. ONE OF THEIR MINIONS KILLED SOMEONE WHO WAS OFF-LIMITS, EVEN ACCORDING TO VAMP LAW. A NUN.

BONSOIR.

BONSOIR. WE APOLOGIZE AGAIN FOR OUR INDISCRETIONS.

WE MEANT NO DISRESPECT.

I DON'T KNOW THE WHOLE STORY. BUT SABINE IS AN OLD BLOOD, KEY TO RADFORD'S POWER BASE. AND PHILIPPE IS HER CONSORT.

WE ARE FAMILY. YOU ARE FORGIVEN.

MERCI, YOUR HIGHNESS!

WE BRING TRIBUTE NOW!

CLAP CLAP

FOR THE MASTER. A KUKRI KNIFE. IT ONCE BELONGED TO JONATHAN HARKER.

IT'S NOT?

IT IS. YOU HOLD ONE OF THE TWO KNIVES THAT KILLED DRACULA PRIME.

THAT IS NOT ALL. WE DID NOT FORGET OUR PRINCESS. SOMETHING SPECIAL FOR YOU.

MIRANDA, I THOUGHT YOU WERE . . . HELP! HELP ME, PLEASE.

IT'S GEOFF CALVO FROM DALLAS. MIRANDA'S UNREQUITED HIGH-SCHOOL CRUSH.

WHAT WILL SHE DO WITH HIM? HERE? NOW?

MERCI. YOUR RESEARCH IS IMPECCABLE, BUT, ALAS, OUTDATED. IN THE PAST YEAR, MY TASTES HAVE CHANGED.

IS SHE TALKING ABOUT ME?

IF WE HAVE DISPLEASED YOU—

IT'S ALL RIGHT. I SEE NO REASON TO MENTION THIS TO THE MASTER. NEXT TIME WE'LL TRY HARDER, WON'T WE?

OUI, YOUR HIGHNESS.

OF COURSE.

PUT THE BOY ON THE ROYAL JET, BOUND FOR DFW AIRPORT. SEE THAT HE IS NOT FURTHER HARMED.

FIRST, THOUGH, I WISH A MOMENT ALONE WITH HIM.

MIRANDA?

HUSH. I'M THINKING.

COOPERATE WITH YOUR ESCORTS AND RETURN HOME. YOU WILL RETAIN NO MEMORY OF THESE EVENTS. CALL YOUR PARENTS. THEY'LL RETRIEVE YOU AT THE AIRPORT.

YOU MAY GO.

HE'S UNDER HER THRALL.

OH, AND ANOTHER THING.

IF YOU EVER CATCH A TALL, GANGLY, B-LIST, GEEKY GIRL STARING AT YOU, BE NICE TO HER. NOTHING FANCY. JUST SAY HI.

AND IF HER NAME IS LUCY LEHMAN, GIVE HER A CHANCE. SHE MIGHT BE BETTER FOR YOU THAN THAT SKANK YOU TOOK TO HOMECOMING.

MIRANDA STILL THINKS ABOUT HER BEST FRIEND. STILL CARES ABOUT HER.

WHAT *IS* IT WITH YOU AND THAT GUY?

IT . . . IT WAS A LONG TIME AGO.

WHY DID YOU LET HIM GO?

WHAT DO YOU THINK, JIMINY CRICKET?

I THINK IT WASN'T A VERY DRAGON-PRINCESS THING TO DO.

I SUGGESTED O'CONNER'S BAR & GRILL BECAUSE THE DALLAS LOCATION OF THE CHAIN WAS ONE OF MIRANDA'S FAVORITES.

WE'RE MEETING FREDDY, THE EVENT PLANNER. IT'S CROWDED. WE DON'T HAVE A RESERVATION.

WE'RE NEXT. TABLE FOR THREE.

TABLE. FOR. THREE.

LOOK OUT, JEDI.

THIS WAY.

NOW, WAIT JUST A MINUTE! WE WERE HERE FIRST!

SORRY, SHE'S GOT A BIG APPETITE.

HISSSSS

FREDDY WILL BE HERE ANY MINUTE, BUT IF YOU'RE STARVING, GO AHEAD AND ORDER.

I'M STILL NEW TO EARTHLY PLEASURES: FOOD, DRINK, SLEEP, SEX, THE BASICS. I DON'T GET ENOUGH SHUT-EYE, AND FORNICATION IS OUT OF THE QUESTION.

IT IS.

NOT EVERYBODY IS ON A LIQUID DIET.

WELCOME TO O'CONNER'S.

YEAH, I'LL HAVE THE VEGGIE QUESADILLAS, CHICKEN NACHOS, SHRIMP FETTUCCINI ALFREDO, THE CORN SUCCOTASH, A LIGHT BEER . . . MAYBE THE CHOCOLATE VOLCANO FOR DESSERT.

WILL THAT BE ALL, DUDE?

JOSHUA.

DUDE?

NO.

HE SHOULDN'T BE HERE. AT LEAST NOT SHOWING HIMSELF. COME TO THINK OF IT, HE SHOULDN'T HAVE SHOWN HIMSELF ON THE TRAIN RIDE UP, EITHER.

I MEAN, YEAH. I MEAN, WE, UH, HAVE SOMEBODY ELSE JOINING US.

WE'LL SPLIT THE QUESADILLAS.

WHAT'S YOUR SECRET?

DID JOSHUA SOMEHOW BLOW MY COVER?

WHAT?

DON'T YOU EVER GAIN WEIGHT? WHEN I WAS A HUMAN, I COULD NEVER EAT LIKE THAT. A WEREHIPPO COULDN'T EAT LIKE THAT.

THERE'S NO SUCH THING AS WEREHIPPOS.

mwah! mwah!

EXCEPT FOR THE BLEACHED HAIR AND GLASSES, FREDDY LOOKS EXACTLY LIKE HARRISON. THEY'RE IDENTICAL TWINS.

WE CAN SCATTER DIME-SIZE RUBIES ON THE BUFFET TABLE OR MAYBE SAPPHIRES IF YOU'RE THINKING RED IS OVERDONE.

SO OVERDONE.

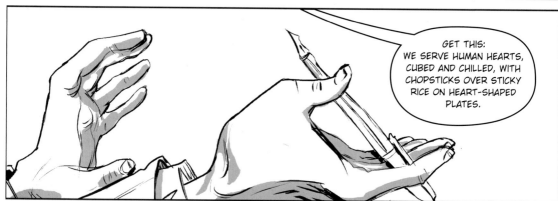

GET THIS: WE SERVE HUMAN HEARTS, CUBED AND CHILLED, WITH CHOPSTICKS OVER STICKY RICE ON HEART-SHAPED PLATES.

OF COURSE, REAL HEARTS AREN'T HEART-SHAPED AT ALL. THEY'RE MORE DISGUSTING AND LUMPY. HENCE THE CUBING, WHICH SOLVES—

I CAN'T LISTEN TO ANY MORE OF THIS.

YOU WANT A DRINK?

I'D LOVE A—

I'LL GET THE WAITER.

WHERE HAVE YOU BEEN?

YOU'RE ASKING ME?

IT'S HARD WORK, WAITING TABLES. THE KITCHEN IS RUNNING SLOW, EVERYBODY WANTS TO SUBSTITUTE SOMETHING, AND HUNGRY PEOPLE CAN BE MEAN.

SINCE WHEN CAN YOU JUST WALK AROUND?

COVERT-OPS EXCEPTION. NO SHOWING OFF THE WINGS, NO LIGHTING UP, BUT . . .

I'M STYLIN'.

ABOUT MIRANDA—

I FIGURED YOU'D BE JAZZED TO SEE HER AGAIN. COOL, HUH?

UH, EXCEPT FOR HER BEING . . . THAT SUCKS. I DON'T MEAN IT SUCKS LIKE . . . SORRY, DUDE. I TOTALLY—

SHUT UP. LISTEN. CAN A VAMPIRE BE SAVED? CAN *I* SAVE HER?

AN ANGEL MAY ENCOURAGE, MAY INSPIRE, MAY NUDGE, BUT EACH HUMAN SOUL ULTIMATELY CHOOSES ITS—

OW!

WE'RE NOT TALKING "HUMAN." DOES *SHE* STILL HAVE A SOUL?

WHAT'S LEFT IS INFECTED. IT'S WITHERING, AND EVERY TIME HER VAMP NATURE KICKS IN, IT'LL WITHER MORE UNTIL THERE'S—

NOTHING LEFT.

I PASS FREDDY ON MY WAY BACK TO THE TABLE.

ABOUT MY BROTHER . . .

FREDDY'S VOICE IS DIFFERENT. THE WAY HE HOLDS HIMSELF.

YOU KNOW HARRISON? YOU WORK WITH HIM?

NOT ANYMORE. HE'S . . .

SO IT'S TRUE.

HE'S AMONG THE UNDEAD.

AFTER LUNCH

WE SHOULD BE GETTING BACK TO THE CASTLE.

WHY? WHAT ARE YOU, A WORKAHOLIC? WHAT DO YOU DO FOR FUN?

I DO NEED TO GET FATHER A GIFT FOR HIS DEATHDAY.

LET'S HIT A BOOKSTORE. OR TWO.

LIKE FATHER RAMOS, SOME LITTLE KIDS CAN RECOGNIZE WHAT I AM.

PARANORMAL
ROMANCE

SELF HELP

Gerbils

DO YOU BELIEVE IN ANGELS?

ANGELS? SEEMS LIKE WISHFUL THINKING.

ANGELS TO ZOM
THE APOCALYPSE
A TO Z

TRY THIS.

WOW THE CROWD
A GUIDE FOR ACTORS

DO YOU WANT TO STOP IN?

LET'S GO DANCING INSTEAD.

I'D LIKE TO TAKE YOU THERE SOMETIME.

HOW ABOUT NEXT WEEK?

WE'RE BOTH ENJOYING THIS, BUT IT CAN'T LAST. DRAC RADFORD WILL RETURN IN JUST UNDER THREE WEEKS.

SWANKY.

UH, DO YOU KNOW HOW TO DANCE?

TWO GLASSES OF SHIRAZ, PLEASE.

I'M SURPRISED HE DIDN'T CARD US. DID YOU USE YOUR MENTAL MOJO ON HIM?

I'LL NEVER LOOK TWENTY-ONE. HOW OLD ARE YOU?

OLD ENOUGH TO KNOW—

WHOA!

SORRY, SIR!

SOME SODA WATER. HURRY!

THAT'S GOOD ENOUGH FOR NOW.

VAROOOOOOOO

WHY DON'T WE STAY AT THE HOTEL TONIGHT?

I DON'T KNOW—

PLEASE. I WANT TO PRETEND LIKE I'M ALIVE.

I'M PLAYING WITH HELLFIRE.

JUST TONIGHT.

WE'D LIKE THE BRIDAL SUITE. THE NAME IS "DRACUL."

NO PROBLEM. IT'S ON THE HOUSE, AND I'LL PUT YOU DOWN FOR A LATE CHECKOUT.

THANK YOU.

DID YOU ENJOY THAT?

DIDN'T YOU? DON'T YOU ASPIRE TO BECOME ETERNAL ROYALTY?

ME?

SHE'S TALKING ABOUT MY BECOMING HER VAMP CONSORT. LIKE PHILIPPE IS TO SABINE.

I CAN'T SAY I'M NOT TEMPTED. ESPECIALLY SINCE LETTING CALVO GO, SHE'S STAYED ON THE ANIMAL BLOOD. PIGS' MOST RECENTLY.

HOW'RE YOU FEELING? YOU'RE LOOKING A LITTLE PALE.

OH, THAT. I SKIPPED DRINKING DINNER BEFORE WE LEFT. I HADN'T BEEN PLANNING TO STAY OUT ALL NIGHT.

ARE YOU GOING TO BE—?

DON'T WORRY. YOU'RE SAFE WITH ME. AT LEAST AS SAFE AS YOU WANT TO BE.

THE BRIDAL SUITE

IN HERE! YOU NEED TO SOAK THAT STAIN.

NO TOUCHING.

WHERE DID THAT COME FROM? THE TATTOO, I MEAN.

AUSTIN.

YOU WERE IN TEXAS? ARE YOU FROM TEXAS?

I WAS IN AUSTIN BEFORE CHICAGO. I WAS IN DALLAS BEFORE THAT.

I'M FROM DALLAS ORIGINALLY.

I ORDER A ROBE, TOO.

I WAS THERE WHEN MIRANDA TOOK HER FIRST BREATH.

ON HER FIRST DAY OF SCHOOL,

AND WHEN SHE HAD THE CHICKEN POX.

IN THE LOCKER ROOM WHEN THE QUEEN BEE MOCKED HER BRA SIZE.

$3x+5$
$=?$

$3x=15$

$\frac{3x}{3}=\frac{15}{3}$

$x=5$

IN ALGEBRA, WHEN SHE MOONED OVER GEOFF CALVO AND GOT A C.

WHEN SHE WROTE *BFF* ON LUCY'S ARM CAST.

BFF!

AND WHEN SHE ADOPTED MR. NESBIT.

I WAS THERE WHEN GRANDPA SHEN WAS BURIED WITH MILITARY HONORS.

WHEN MIRANDA CHICKENED OUT OF RIDING THE ROLLER COASTER.

AND WHEN HER PARENTS ANNOUNCED THAT THEIR MARRIAGE HAD GONE BUST.

THE NIGHT AT THE MOVIE THEATER WHEN I REALIZED THAT I DIDN'T JUST LOVE HER. I WAS *IN* LOVE WITH HER, TOO.

BOX OFF

IT DOESN'T FEEL WRONG.

IT'S ONE THING TO DIE A VIRGIN. IT'S ANOTHER TO BE AN UNDEAD ONE.

WHAT DID SHE JUST SAY?

FORGET LOVE. FORGET PASSION. NO WAY SHOULD I DEFLOWER THE UNDEAD.

WHAT'S WRONG?

I'M SORRY. I SHOULDN'T HAVE . . .

IT'S BECAUSE OF WHAT I AM, ISN'T IT?

I KNOW YOU'VE DONE TERRIBLE THINGS. BUT HAVE YOU CONSIDERED THAT YOU COULD STILL BE—?

SAVED? PICK SOMEONE ELSE TO PROSELYTIZE TO.

MIRANDA, PLEASE! LET'S JUST—

OVER THE NEXT WEEK . . .

ST. BE...SHE...

WOULD YOU LIKE GRAVY WITH THAT?

I'M NOT FOOLING MYSELF.

THERE WERE A MILLION THINGS I COULD'VE SAID, DONE WHEN MIRANDA TOSSED ME OUT.

BUT I'M THE ONE WHO INITIATED THE FIRST KISS.

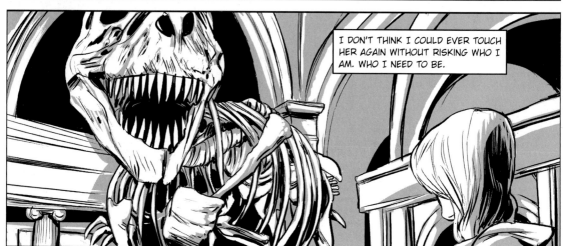

I DON'T THINK I COULD EVER TOUCH HER AGAIN WITHOUT RISKING WHO I AM. WHO I NEED TO BE.

WHAT DO YOU WANT?

IT'S BEEN A WEEK. WHAT IS THIS, INTERMISSION? ARE YOU JUST GONNA GIVE UP?

SHE FIRED ME. IT'S OVER.

SHE FIRED YOU? DID YOU FORGET WHO YOU'RE WORKING FOR? OR DID YOU CHANGE SIDES?

YOU KNOW WHAT HAPPENED. YOU KNOW WHAT I MEAN.

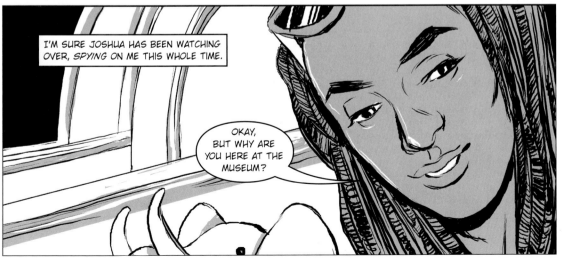

I'M SURE JOSHUA HAS BEEN WATCHING OVER, *SPYING* ON ME THIS WHOLE TIME.

OKAY, BUT WHY ARE YOU HERE AT THE MUSEUM?

MOST SELF-RESPECTING ANGELS WOULD'VE CHOSEN A RELIGIOUS REFUGE. LIKE A CHURCH, A SYNAGOGUE, A TEMPLE, WRIGLEY FIELD.

MAMMALS OF ASIA

I'M SURPRISED IT TOOK HIM THIS LONG TO START NAGGING.

WHAT ABOUT YOUR MISSION?

WELL, LET'S SEE. I'M POWERLESS. NO WINGS, NO RADIANCE. BUT BIG DEAL.

SO WHAT IF I'M PERSONA NON GRATA AT THE CASTLE. ALL I HAVE TO DO IS SMITE DRAC RADFORD . . .

AND SAVE MIRANDA'S SOUL, EVEN THOUGH SHE LITERALLY THREW ME OUT OF HER AFTERLIFE.

IS THAT ALL?

I KNOW, I KNOW. I'VE ALSO GOT TO FREE THE PRISONERS.

90

DESPITE THE WOLF-FORM VAMP SENTRIES . . .

THE TWELVE-FOOT IRON FENCE . . .

AND A NEIGHBORHOOD CHOCK-FULL OF BLOODSUCKERS.

WHITE ESTA

EXCELLENT!

DUDE, THAT'S SO AMBITIOUS!

BUT IS IT POSSIBLE? ABOUT MIRANDA, I MEAN. HER SOUL. CAN SHE BE SAVED?

UH, THERE'S SOMETHING YOU SHOULD KNOW.

JUST TELL ME.

YOU'RE NOT TOTALLY WITHOUT HOPE. YOU'VE STILL GOT YOUR LOOKS, YOUR SEX APPEAL (OR WHAT PASSES FOR IT), YOUR IMMORTALITY, AND—THIS IS KEY—YOUR INFLUENCE.

"ANGEL ON MY SHOULDER" AND ALL THAT CRAP. SO?

HEAVEN ITSELF IS ROOTING FOR YOU.

BUT FOR THE LAST WEEK, MIRANDA'S BEEN HANDLING THE VAMPIRE THING ON HER OWN.

I'M AFRAID TO ASK WHAT SHE'S DONE.

AND IT'S NOT LIKE SHE VAMPED OUT YESTERDAY.

ROOM SERVICE!

HELLO?

SHE'S COMMITTED SOME SERIOUS WRONGS.

AND YOU CAN'T SAVE SOMEONE ELSE.

IT HAS TO BE HER DECISION.

SHE HAS TO CHOOSE TO DO WHAT'S RIGHT.

FROM WHERE I STAND, IT'S TOO CLOSE TO CALL. TONIGHT'S PARTY—

WHAT DO YOU MEAN *TONIGHT'S?* DRAC RADFORD'S SUPPOSED TO BE ON A JET TO . . . I DON'T KNOW . . . SYDNEY RIGHT NOW!

WE RELY ON TRAVEL ITINERARIES PROVIDED BY THE DARK MASTER SINCE WHEN?

GIVE ME YOUR PHONE!

FATHER RAMOS?

CHURCH PARKING LOT

THE PRIEST GAVE ME THE FLAMETHROWERS, THE BACKPACK FULL OF STAKES.

I CAN DRIVE AND—

SORRY, FATHER. THIS IS A SOLO MISSION.

STAY HERE. STAY SAFE.

YOU'RE SURE THERE'S NOTHING ELSE I CAN DO?

PRAY.

FORTUNATELY, I'M REALLY GOOD AT THAT.

WE WILL NEVER MAKE IT OVER THE FENCE.

I JUST DROVE IN, AND LEFT THE FRONT GATE OPEN BEHIND ME.

I'D RATHER DIE FIGHTING THAN—

I'LL SHOW YOU HOW TO USE A FLAMETHROWER.

TAKE IT EASY.

YOU'VE GOT WEAPONS?

TWO FLAMETHROWERS, STAKES FOR EVERYONE. I BROUGHT WHAT I COULD CARRY.

HOW MANY VAMPIRES ARE IN THE CASTLE?

WHERE DO THEY SLEEP?

THAT GIRL, SHE WON'T LEAVE HER BROTHER. BUT THE TRADERS WHO SOLD HIM BROKE HIS LEG. HE CAN'T WALK.

SO THEY DIE. SOME OF US WILL, NO MATTER WHAT.

LADIES AND GENTLEMEN, YOUR ODDS JUST GOT A LOT BETTER.

WELCOME HOME, ZACHARY. HER HIGHNESS HASN'T BEEN THE SAME WITHOUT YOU.

I DON'T BLAME LAURIE FOR TURNING ME IN. BUT IF SHE AND NORA HAVE ALERTED THE SENTRIES, WE'RE SCREWED.

YOU'LL NEVER MAKE IT TO THE FRONT GATE ON FOOT. NOT ALL OF YOU.

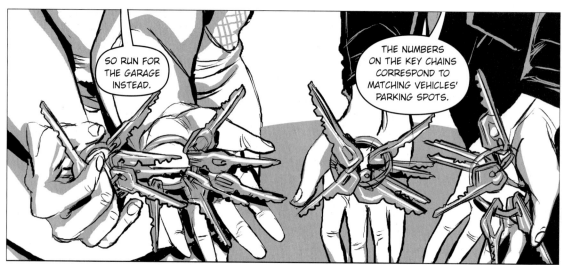

SO RUN FOR THE GARAGE INSTEAD.

THE NUMBERS ON THE KEY CHAINS CORRESPOND TO MATCHING VEHICLES' PARKING SPOTS.

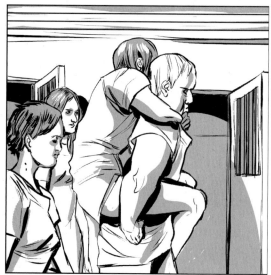

I WANT TO STAY. FIGHT.

GET THE WEAKER ONES TO SAFETY. THEY'RE MORE IMPORTANT.

ABOUT THAT WHOLE "DAMN-YOU" THING . . .

DON'T SWEAT IT.

WE'D BEST GET A MOVE ON, TOO. THE MASTER WILL REALIZE WE HAD A HAND IN THIS. WE DON'T HAVE MUCH TIME.

WE'LL TAKE MY BUG.

AROOOOOOOOOOoooo
ARRRROooooooo

SENTRIES.

YOU TWO GO! THERE'S SOMETHING ELSE I HAVE TO DO HERE.

MRRAAWWHHHHHHHHH

AND THAT WAS BRENEK.

IF YOU'RE STAYING, I'M STAYING. LAURIE, GO AHEAD WITHOUT US.

BUT—

BUT NOTHING. I'M NOT SURE HOW MANY OF THOSE KIDS EVEN KNOW HOW TO DRIVE.

SO FAR, MY MISSION IS A SUCCESS. AND NOW I HAVE AN ALLY IN NORA.

FEELING GOOD ABOUT YOURSELF, AREN'T YOU?

HUMAN HARRISON WOULD NEVER HURT NORA. WITH VAMPIRE HARRISON, I'M NOT SO SURE.

NO USE. I'D NEVER STRIKE IN TIME.

STOMP!

OOPH!

AND MY BLEEDING STOCK!

MY INSTINCT IS TO ARGUE WITH ANYTHING HE SAYS. BUT I'M KIND OF PROUD OF DOING ALL THAT.

NORA, WE'RE EXPECTING GUESTS. GO UPSTAIRS, GET TO THE KITCHEN, AND DO YOUR JOB.

HARRISON, CHAIN MY DAUGHTER'S MISTAKE. GIVE ME FIFTEEN MINUTES, AND THEN ESCORT HIM TO THE PARLOR. IT'S TIME THE YOUNG LOVERS WERE REUNITED, DON'T YOU THINK?

HE'LL MAKE A PERFECT AMUSE-BOUCHE.

I THINK THAT MEANS "TINY APPETIZER." I'M NOT ONLY FOOD, I'M INSULTED.

YOUR MAJESTY, I'M LIKE YOU NOW, A BLESSED BEING. IT WAS I WHO ROOTED OUT THIS DECEPTION—

WHO ARE *YOU* TO SPEAK OF BETRAYAL?

THE MASTER WILL KILL NORA FOR THIS. KILL HER TRULY DEAD. WHAT WERE YOU THINKING?

NORA MADE HER OWN DECISION. NORA CHOSE WELL.

I DON'T HAVE THE SPEED OR STRENGTH TO GET AWAY.

WHY DID YOU BAIL ON DRAC, ANYWAY?

HE KEPT PUTTING OFF MY ELEVATION. YOU TURN FORTY, YOU THINK ABOUT LIVING FOREVER, AND YOU WONDER IF YOU'LL BE AS PRETTY IF YOUR LOOKS ARE FROZEN AT FORTY-THREE.

SO, WHO WAS IT? WHO TURNED YOU?

DELTA.

HUH?

CL/NK

DELTA THE SENTRY. THE MASTER CALLS THEM ALPHA, BETA, GAMMA—

TALK ABOUT DEHUMANIZING. I MEAN, EVEN IF THEY ARE—

INHUMAN? YES, DELTA MADE THAT VERY POINT.

WHERE HAVE YOU BEEN ALL THIS TIME?

MADISON.

AN UNDERGROUND SPA RESORT OWNED BY ROGUE ETERNALS. I SIGNED UP FOR THE "ALL-ME, ALL-NIGHT" PACKAGE. THAT'S A FACIAL, A SWEDISH MASSAGE, AND AN HERBAL BLOOD WRAP.

I JUST HAD TO ASK.

DING

MIRANDA?

IF MICHAEL HADN'T YANKED MY POWERS, I COULD USE MY RADIANCE. LIGHT UP LIKE A SUPERNOVA AND DESTROY DRAC RADFORD.

EXCEPT MIRANDA WOULD ALSO BE DIRECTLY EXPOSED. I CAN'T BRING MYSELF TO GIVE UP ON MY GIRL. NOT YET. EVEN IF SHE IS IGNORING ME.

BESIDES, HARRISON MAY BE REDEEMABLE, TOO.

Bzzz Bzzz

HARRISON HERE!

EXCUSE ME, PLEASE.

PRESENTING SABINE, PHILIPPE, AND GEOFF.

IT'S GEOFF CALVO, MIRANDA'S HIGH-SCHOOL HEARTTHROB, ONLY THIS TIME WITH FANGS.

THEY DEFIED MIRANDA'S ORDERS, FED HIM DEMONIC BLOOD, AND KILLED HIM.

THE MASTER INFORMED US THAT YOU WOULD RECONSIDER HIM AS A CONSORT.

DEAR BOY, WE HAVE A SURPRISE FOR YOU TONIGHT. THIS . . .

IS HER HIGHNESS'S FORMER PERSONAL ASSISTANT. HE HAS BEEN DISCHARGED.

IN HONOR OF YOUR INTRODUCTION TO ETERNAL SOCIETY, I INVITE YOU TO TAKE THE FIRST BITE.

I'M GOING TO HELL. AND THIS IS THE WELCOMING COMMITTEE.

FATHER—

NEVER FEAR, SUGAR PLUM. YOU'RE WELCOME TO FINISH THE TRAITOR OFF.

MY ANGELIC BLOOD!
DRINKING IT DESTROYED HIM.

WHAT WAS THAT, A PROTECTION SPELL? WHAT ARE YOU? A SORCERER, A WARLOCK, *WHAT?*

I'M ON A MISSION FROM GOD.

THAT NIGHT AT THE CEMETERY, IT WAS YOU. I MEANT TO ADOPT THE OTHER GIRL. BUT WHEN YOU APPEARED TO MIRANDA, I KNEW SHE MUST BE SPECIAL.

HA! FULLY ENDOWED ANGELS DON'T TEND TO SPEND QUALITY TIME WITH ETERNALS. EVEN DAUGHTER-SEDUCING DO-GOODERS LIKE THIS ONE.

WELL, YES, BUT—

IF HE WEREN'T FALLEN, HE WOULD'VE ALREADY VANISHED TO THE CELESTIAL PLANE OR USED HIS RADIANCE TO VAPORIZE US.

HE'S A GUARDIAN ANGEL?

YEAH. I AM, OR AT LEAST I WAS, YOURS.

REMOVE HIM TO THE MAIN COURTYARD. HE'LL MAKE FINE ENTERTAINMENT.

YOU CAN'T KILL ME.

I KNOW. IT MAKES YOU THE PERFECT, PERPETUAL VICTIM. I'LL PUBLICLY TORTURE YOU, NIGHT AFTER NIGHT, YEAR AFTER YEAR, FOR CENTURIES.

I'VE NEVER FELT SO HELPLESS, STUPID, OR RIDICULOUS IN MY ENTIRE LIFE.

I LIKE IT.

PUHTEWWH

I LIKE THE DRAMA, THE COMPOSITION. AN ANGEL, YOU SAY?

A FALLEN ANGEL.

FOOLISH, FALLEN ANGEL.

YOU KNEW FIRSTHAND ABOUT THE DEMONIC. WHY WOULDN'T YOU BELIEVE IN US?

WE WERE RAISED IN THIS WORLD, FREDDY AND I, CHILDREN OF SERVANTS WHO WERE CHILDREN OF SERVANTS.

YOUR BROTHER DOESN'T WANT TO VAMP OUT—

NO, HE WOULD'VE RUN FROM THIS LIFE LONG AGO . . .

IF IT WEREN'T FOR YOU.

YOU'RE LUCKY THIS ONE SHOWED UP, HARRISON. THE MASTER'S ORIGINAL PLAN WAS TO PUT *YOU* INTO THE HOLY-WATER DUNKING TANK.

YOU HAVE A LITTLE ANGEL TATTOOED ON YOUR CHEST. A CHERUB.

THAT IS NOT ONE OF THE *CHERUBIM.* THAT IS A FAT, NAKED WHITE BABY WITH WINGS.

HE IS AN ANGEL FALLEN—STRIPPED OF FLIGHT AND RADIANCE—BUT STILL IN THE SERVICE OF THE OPPOSITION.

SUGAR.

MMMPPPHH!

I CAN'T BELIEVE SHE'D REALLY . . .

LOOK THIS WAY! EXALTED MASTER, PRINCESS CUTIE. FRENCHIES!

GAHKKKH—

ASSHRRGH

YOU'RE BLEEDING.

RADFORD CUT ME. A PUNISHMENT. BUT IT'S NOT DEEP, AND I HEAL FAST. FASTER THAN A HUMAN.

YOU'RE SURE?

WE'LL TALK LATER.

LOOKS LIKE MOST OF THE MONSTERS BACK MIRANDA. OR AT LEAST SABINE.

WEREBEARS. THEY'RE TEARING INTO ANY VAMP THEY CAN.

SPLISH

THE DUNGEON ESCAPEES! WITH HOLY-WATER BALLOONS!

EEEAHHHCKH!

BEATS ME IF I'M REINSTATED. BUT THE WINGS HAVE TO BE A GOOD SIGN.

ONCE AGAIN, I CAN FEEL THE POWER TO RADIATE HEAVEN'S LIGHT. BUT NOT WITH MIRANDA OUT IN THE OPEN LIKE THAT. IT WOULD DESTROY HER.

THE CROWD IS AWED BY MY HOLY WINGS.

ROOOAAAAAARRRR!!!

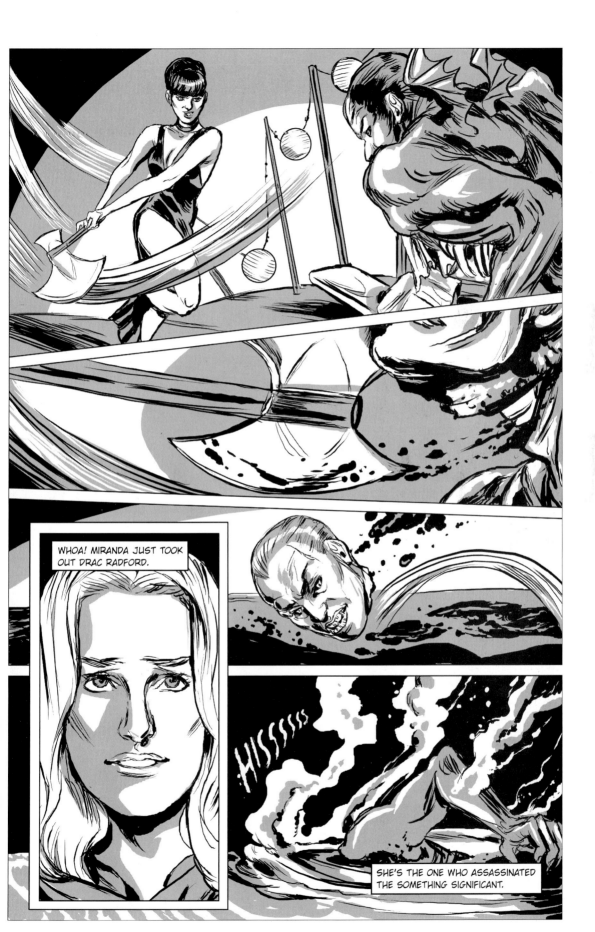

WHOA! MIRANDA JUST TOOK OUT DRAC RADFORD.

HISSSSSss

SHE'S THE ONE WHO ASSASSINATED THE SOMETHING SIGNIFICANT.

LET IT BE KNOWN THAT THE WEREBEARS AND ALL HUMANS ON THIS PROPERTY ARE UNDER MY PERSONAL PROTECTION.

ANY OF THE BEARS OR VAMPS COULD KICK MY ASS. PROBABLY A COUPLE OF THE HUMANS, TOO. BUT THEY DON'T HAVE TO KNOW THAT.

BEST DAMN GALA I'VE EVER BEEN TO.

WHAT THE HELL JUST HAPPENED?

I'M THE SCARIEST VAMPIRE IN THE WORLD. I'M THE NEW DRACULA.

TURNS OUT THE OTHER TWO BEARS ARE BRENEK'S PARENTS.

THE DUNGEON BREAK WENT WELL. SOME MINOR INJURIES, BUT ZERO FATALITIES ON OUR SIDE.

IF YOU EVER NEED ANYTHING . . . SERIOUSLY. STANDING OFFER.

ALL THE KIDS ARE SAFE.

EVERYONE WHO NEEDED MEDICAL TREATMENT IS RECEIVING IT.

HERE'S CONTACT INFO FOR A PRIEST WHO'S A PAL OF MINE. HE SHOULD BE ABLE TO HELP GET EVERYBODY HOME. OR SOMEPLACE BETTER.

FATHER RAMOS †

NOW, I'LL JUST POP OVER TO THE CASTLE AND—

I CAN'T. ALL IS NOT FORGIVEN. I CAN'T TRANSPORT MYSELF AT WILL. I'M STILL STUCK ON THE MORTAL PLANE.

WHAT ARE YOU DOING?

SKRITCH SKRITCH

SKRITCH SKRITCH

THUMP

IS THIS WHY YOU TOOK OUT DRAC RADFORD, SO YOU COULD BECOME THE BIGGEST, BADDEST VAMP OF ALL?

YOU WERE MY GUARDIAN ANGEL. SO YOU WATCHED ME ALL THE TIME? LIKE WHEN I GOT MY PERIOD OR DOCTORED A ZIT OR TOOK A SHOWER?

I'M AN ANGEL, NOT A PEEPING TOM.

ACTUALLY, SHOWER TIME WAS ONE OF MY FAVORITES.

I KNEW WHAT I WAS DOING THEN.

SORT OF.

AND I KNOW WHAT I'M DOING NOW! I'M NOT THE DRACULA ANYMORE. I JUST ABDICATED THE MANTLE TO SABINE. PHILIPPE SIGNED THE DECREE AS MY WITNESS.

OH. SORRY.

WHY HAVE A DRACULA AT ALL?

UNTIL THE LAST VAMPIRE FADES AWAY, THE DRACULA IS NECESSARY FOR ORDER. IF THERE'S A POWER VACUUM, THERE'LL BE AN UNDEAD FREE-FOR-ALL.

UNTIL THE LAST VAMPIRE FADES AWAY?

OUR LAWS AND TRADITIONS DON'T EXIST WITHOUT REASON. ULTIMATELY, THEY PROTECT THE HUMANS AS MUCH AS THEY DO US.

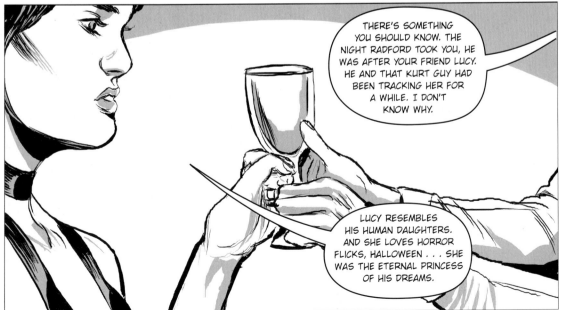

THERE'S SOMETHING YOU SHOULD KNOW. THE NIGHT RADFORD TOOK YOU, HE WAS AFTER YOUR FRIEND LUCY. HE AND THAT KURT GUY HAD BEEN TRACKING HER FOR A WHILE. I DON'T KNOW WHY.

LUCY RESEMBLES HIS HUMAN DAUGHTERS. AND SHE LOVES HORROR FLICKS, HALLOWEEN . . . SHE WAS THE ETERNAL PRINCESS OF HIS DREAMS.

WHEN I APPEARED, HE CHANGED HIS PLANS. AND TOOK YOU INSTEAD.

OH, THANK YOU! THANK YOU SO MUCH!

SHE'S CRACKED. I'VE PUSHED HER OVER THE EDGE.

DO YOU UNDERSTAND WHAT I'M SAYING?

YES!

MWAH!

MWAH!

YOU SAVED LUCY. SHE'S MY BEST FRIEND, THE ONLY CLOSE FRIEND I HAD BEFORE YOU.

FEW HUMANS WOULD BE SO SELFLESS. WHATEVER MY GIRL IS, WHATEVER SHE'S DONE, HOW COULD THE BIG BOSS REJECT HER?

HOW CAN I?

MEET ME IN THE COURTYARD. SAY, TEN MINUTES?

WHAT'S YOUR PLEASURE?

I HAVE A FAVOR TO ASK. TWO ACTUALLY.

ANYTHING.

YOU'RE STUCK ON EARTH?

I USED TO THINK SO. THAT I WAS STUCK. NOW, THERE'S NOWHERE ELSE I'D RATHER BE.

GUARDIAN ANGELS HELP PEOPLE.

WE TRY. THERE ARE LIMITS. BUT YEAH, WE DO OUR BEST.

COULD YOU HELP VAMPIRES LIKE ME, IF THEY'RE NOT TOO FAR GONE? IF THEY HAVE SOME SOUL STILL LEFT?

ULTIMATELY, EACH WILL HAVE TO DECIDE HIS OR HER OWN FATE. BUT YES, IF THAT'S WHAT YOU WANT, I'LL DO WHAT I CAN.

ABOUT THE OTHER FAVOR. I CAN'T BE THIS THING ANYMORE.

WE'LL TAKE IT ONE NIGHT—

NO. I'M WALKING, I'M TALKING, BUT ZACHARY . . . I'M DEAD. I HAVE BEEN FOR A WHILE.

YOU'RE NOT THAT . . . I MEAN—

YOU KNOW THE MAIDS? I'M THE REASON THEIR TONGUES WERE CUT OUT.

WHY DON'T YOU BITE ME, LIKE CALVO DID, AND BE DONE WITH IT?

BECAUSE THAT'S NOT WHO WE ARE. YOU THINK THAT . . . I'M GOING TO HELL, AREN'T I?

I DON'T KNOW. IT'S NOT UP TO ME.

MIRANDA'S SOUL. SHE DID IT! SHE SAVED HERSELF. MICHAEL'S TAKING HER TO HEAVEN.

YOU HAVE FULFILLED YOUR MISSION. YOU HAVE DONE WELL.

MY MISSION?

JOSH SAID I WAS SUPPOSED TO WIPE OUT SOMETHING OF TREMENDOUS SIGNIFICANCE. RADFORD, I'D ASSUMED.

COULD HE HAVE MEANT *MIRANDA*?

For Kathi —
teacher, friend, sister, angel,
herder of cats
C. L. S.

For Neil, for everything
M. D.

This is a work of fiction. Names, characters, places, and incidents are either
products of the author's imagination or, if real, are used fictitiously.

Text copyright © 2013 by Cynthia Leitich Smith
Interior illustrations copyright © 2013 by Ming Doyle

First edition 2013

Library of Congress Catalog Card Number 2012942385
ISBN 978-0-7636-5119-0

12 13 14 15 16 17 QGD 10 9 8 7 6 5 4 3 2 1

Printed in Dubuque, Iowa, U.S.A.

This book was typeset in CCWildWords.
The illustrations were done in ink.

Candlewick Press
99 Dover Street
Somerville, Massachusetts 02144

visit us at www.candlewick.com

Author's Note

I believe in angels—both literal and metaphorical. When I decided to create a fantastical world with prowling monsters, I knew there must be angels in the mix, too. And there's something fierce and awesome about an angel with a sword.

The guardian angel (GA) Zachary is my most popular character to date. He makes huge mistakes despite the best of intentions. He's a young man of action who struggles to impress his boss, and he cares deeply for the people in his life, especially his girl, Miranda.

You can further explore their love story in the *Eternal* prose novel, which includes scenes from her point of view, and follow them forward in *Blessed* and *Diabolical*.

Eternal has its literary roots in Abraham Stoker's *Dracula* (1897), Charles Dickens's *A Tale of Two Cities* (1859) and Shakespeare's *Romeo and Juliet* (1597). Readers of my previous graphic novel, *Tantalize: Kieren's Story*, who studiously explore the pages of *Eternal: Zachary's Story*, may spot another key hero from the series in the illustrations.

Here's to the heavenly team at Candlewick Press: editor Deborah Noyes Wayshak, her assistant Carter Hasegawa, and designer Sherry Fatla. Cheers also to my rockin' GAs at Curtis Brown Ltd.: agent Ginger Knowlton and her assistant Mina Feig. My enthusiastic applause to cover illustrator Sam Weber—your Kieren and Zachary are gorgeous. If only you could see YA readers swoon.

Most of all, thank you to the brilliant and talented Ming Doyle. Your vision, care, and formidable talent shine through every panel of both of our books. I'm wowed by you.

Illustrator's Note

After spending a year first with Kieren and Quincie and then another with Zachary and Miranda, I feel like I've been on one of the most glamorous, dangerous, and romantic adventures possible, and all it took was a gallon of ink!

I am eternally (ha!) grateful to Deborah Noyes Wayshak, Carter Hasegawa, and especially Sherry Fatla at Candlewick Press for their unwavering support and involvement. Never could I hope to find a better or more superheroically dedicated team to work with on not one, but two such dark, fun, and thrilling books! My talented and exceedingly patient boyfriend, Neil Cicierega, also went above and beyond the call of duty when it came to rendering technical assistance, providing moral support, and procuring the occasional direly needed cup of midnight coffee.

And of course, as always, my greatest admiration belongs to Cynthia. Thanks for all the dishy characters!

ALSO BY BEST-SELLING AUTHOR CYNTHIA LEITICH SMITH:

Tantalize: Kieren's Story
GRAPHIC NOVEL ILLUSTRATED BY MING DOYLE

"This format- and genre-blending story delivers on several counts as a vampire-werewolf adventure, a mystery, a romance with teeth and claws, an authentic look at diversity (both ethnic and species), and a darn good read." — *Booklist*

Paperback with flaps ISBN 978-0-7636-4114-6

Tantalize
Are you predator or prey? The novel that started it all . . .

"Smith juices up YA horror with this intoxicating romantic thriller." — *The Horn Book*

Hardcover ISBN 978-0-7636-2791-1
Paperback ISBN 978-0-7636-4059-0
E-book ISBN 978-07636-5152-7

Eternal
At last, Miranda is the life of the party.
All she had to do was die.

A *New York Times* Bestseller

"A true page-turner." — *Dallas Morning News*

Hardcover ISBN 978-0-7636-3573-2
Paperback ISBN 978-0-7636-4773-5
E-book ISBN 978-0-7636-5153-4

Blessed
Quincie P. Morris is in the fight of her life—or undeath—as the casts of *Tantalize* and *Eternal* unite for a clash with the ultimate bloodsucker.

"A hearty meal for the thinking vampire reader."
— *The Horn Book*

Hardcover ISBN 978-0-7636-4326-3
Paperback ISBN 978-0-7636-5479-5
E-book ISBN 978-0-7636-5448-1

Diabolical
When heroes from the previous three novels unite to investigate an ominous New England boarding school, the result is an action-packed clash between the forces of heaven and hell.

"A great finish to an original and satisfying series."
— *School Library Journal*

Hardcover ISBN 978-0-7636-5118-3
Paperback ISBN 978-0-7636-6143-4
E-book ISBN 978-0-7636-5963-9